4

JoJo & BowBow

SLUMBER PARTY SPARKLES

BY JoJo Siwa

nickelodeon

AMULET BOOKS
NEW YORK

Cataloging-in-Publication Data has been applied for and may be obtained from the Library of Congress.

ISBN 978-1-4197-4328-3
ebook ISBN 978-1-68335-795-7

Text copyright © 2019 JoJo Siwa
Cover and illustrations copyright © 2019 Abrams Books
Book design by Siobhan Gallagher

Printed and bound in the United States
10 9 8 7 6 5 4 3 2 1

Amulet Books are available at special discounts when purchased in quantity for premiums and promotions as well as fundraising or educational use. Special editions can also be created to specification. For details, contact specialsales@abramsbooks.com or the address below.

ABRAMS The Art of Books
195 Broadway, New York, NY 10007
abramsbooks.com

CONTENTS

CHAPTER 1

"I've gotta be honest," JoJo told her best friend, lifting a doughnut decorated to look like a panda bear to her lips. "Doughnut Planning is definitely my favorite activity."

"Doughnut Planning" was how JoJo and Miley liked to discuss any official matters of business. Miley had gotten the idea from seeing her mom plan breakfast meetings for work—but JoJo and Miley had decided to substitute doughnuts in for bagels for their own meetings, because true businesswomen should be well-sugared, *especially* before school.

The item on today's agenda: Miley's birthday. It was twelve days away, and the girls were tasked with planning the best party ever. After all, it wasn't just any birthday. Miley was about to turn *double digits*. After that came preteen. And then, well . . . *teen*. They had some big life stages ahead of them, and double digits was just the kickoff.

"So I know for sure I want it to be sparkle themed," Miley said, leaning over the booth to pull a glazed cruller from the doughnut spread onto her plate.

"Love it. Sparkles, check." JoJo scribbled the word on her agenda, which was—not coincidentally—covered in sparkles. JoJo and Miley loved sparkles the way some girls loved puppies. If JoJo was being honest, they really loved puppies too. And dance. And candy. And—

"Hello? Earth to JoJo," Miley said, snapping her fingers in front of JoJo's face, which, JoJo realized, probably had an expression as glazed as the doughnuts. She giggled at her private joke.

"Sorry! What did you say?"

"Ice skating!" Miley said, hopping up and down in her seat. "I'm going to have an ice-skating party this year!"

"Um, did I miss something?" JoJo wanted to know. "What does ice skating have to do with sparkles? And have you ever ice-skated in your life? We live in California!"

"So my mom made me watch this movie with her the other night from when she was a kid," Miley explained between bites of cruller. "And at first I was like, 'Mom, lame, they didn't even have movies in HD when you

3

were my age.' But then I watched it because usually my mom knows what I like, and it was *awesome*."

JoJo grinned at her friend. Miley's enthusiasm was contagious. "What was it?" JoJo asked. JoJo's mom always had great taste in movies too. Just like Miley and her mom, they were BFFs.

"*The Cutting Edge!*" shouted Miley. Miley's mom smiled at the girls from where she was sitting a few tables away, eating her own doughnut with a mug of hot coffee. She always "tagged along"—as she called it—to Doughnut Planning, but she made sure to give the girls their privacy. Mrs. McKenna was big on independence—and it showed. Miley was as independent as it got!

"It's so, so good!" Miley exclaimed, sitting taller. "You would *love* it. It's about this hockey player guy who starts figure skating with this really stubborn girl—you should see her costumes, JoJo, they're so pretty, except they could definitely use some more sparkles." Miley paused to take a long sip of OJ. "And they fight the whole time because they both hate each other at first, but of course it's just a front for how much they're totally *in love* with each other . . ."

"Spoiler alert," said JoJo. "Thanks a lot— what if I wanted to watch it?"

"Oh, you will anyway," Miley informed her. "We'll watch it together. And then we'll watch all three sequels, because of course. Toe pick!" Miley squealed, then dissolved in laughter.

"Toe pick?" JoJo had no idea what Miley was talking about. Miley did this sometimes. It was probably the most frustrating part of their friendship. JoJo wanted in on the jokes!

"Miley, you're going to have to explain that one," JoJo told her friend.

"It's just this funny part of the movie that you'll get when you see it," Miley explained. "It's this thing the girl skater always says because the guy skater is always forgetting to use his toe pick—that's a brake on an ice skate—and falling on his face on the ice."

"Got it." JoJo figured she'd *really* get it when she saw the movie. "So this movie made you want to have your birthday party at an ice-skating rink?"

"Totally," said Miley, brushing her long, dark curly hair over one shoulder. "The thing is, the choreography is amazing in figure skating and ice dancing! It made me realize— maybe there's a whole world of choreography to explore beyond just dance."

"Hold the phone. There's a world beyond dance?" JoJo joked, raising her eyebrows in faux-shock. Miley was the most talented choreographer she knew. She'd even choreographed a lot of dances for JoJo! Dance was definitely her thing.

"I'm not saying there's a world beyond dance," Miley clarified. "I'm saying the world *of* dance is bigger than I ever imagined. Just think, JoJo—dancing on the ice, twirling around in sparkly skirts paired with sparkly tights . . ."

"It sounds like you like ice fashion more than ice skating," JoJo teased.

"Ice *dancing*," Miley corrected her. "And I think I'm going to love it all. Which is why I want to start my second decade on the ice with all my favorite people. Ohhh, speaking of fashion—can you imagine the amazing ice-dancing costumes Kyra could make? I bet they'd be even better than the ones in the movie." Their friend Kyra lived in the same neighborhood as Miley and JoJo, and she had incredible fashion sense. Lately she'd been designing her own clothing!

"Girls," Miley's mom called from across the (mostly) empty room. "We've got ten minutes before we have to leave."

"Okay," Miley said, then groaned. "I don't want to go to school! I want to be home-schooled like you, JoJo. You get to do what you want all day long."

"Miley, that isn't true! Do you even know how jealous I get sometimes that you and Kyra and Grace and Jacob get to hang out all day without me? I love my life and I love that being homeschooled allows me to do more songs and go on tour and stuff like that, but sometimes I just miss seeing my crew. And being homeschooled is exhausting! I do my work and then I have to do my other work—

vlogs and voice lessons and performances. It's fun and I love it, but it's hard work!"

"Fair point," said Miley. "School isn't so bad."

JoJo smiled. "Now, focus!" she told her friend. "We're supposed to be planning!"

"Grace already offered to design the invites," Miley said. "So we can rest easy on that one—they'll obviously be insanely cute."

"Definitely," JoJo agreed. "Grace is so talented. She said she was going to make a piñata too."

"A unicorn?" Miley wanted to know. Not only was their friend Grace an amazing artist, she was also a lifelong unicorn fanatic.

"Actually, no." JoJo cleared her throat. "Lately she's been into caticorns."

"Random. But cute!" Miley clapped her hands. "I love caticorns!"

JoJo nodded in agreement. Cats with unicorn horns were very cute, fluffy, cuddly mythical creatures. Anyway, it was high time Grace's unicorns got an update.

"Yes. So she's making a caticorn piñata," JoJo said.

"Love it. What will it be filled with?" Miley asked.

"That part's a surprise, birthday girl! But definitely plan on lots of glitter. And guess what else?" JoJo switched to an orange glitter pen from a pink one, and ran down the list. "Kyra's designing us matching outfits," she said, "and I'll make sure they're bedazzled, since you want a sparkle-themed skating party. Maybe my mom can help with that." JoJo's mom was a pro at bedazzling.

"That's so, so fun," Miley said. "I love it. Kyra is the most fashion-forward girl I know. I'm sure they'll be perfect."

"Yep, we'll come up with a cute hashtag too," JoJo said. "In case we want to post anything on Instagram. Mileystone, maybe? Like, hashtag, Miley's Milestone?"

"Mmmm . . ." Miley paused. "That's super fun, but I think we can do better," she responded, with her usual tact. "You'll think of something perfect. And what about Jacob? Can he handle the cake?"

"Actually, I'm not sure about that," JoJo said. Miley's face fell in disappointment. "He wants to. It's just that he's in the California Junior Pastry Chefs competition the day after your party. Two winners become California Junior Master Pastry Chef or California Junior Sous Pastry Chef and get college scholarships and also get to go to the national contest. He has to do a lot of prep for it. I know he wanted to make your cake, though."

"What! That's so cool!" Miley's face lit up. One of JoJo's favorite things about her friend was her irrepressible enthusiasm for her other friends' talents. "I can't believe he didn't tell me!"

"He literally just texted me this morning," JoJo explained. "Oops! I hope I didn't ruin anything. He may have wanted to tell you in person today at school."

"I'll act surprised," said Miley with a wink. Just then, her mom appeared, sliding into the booth next to Miley.

"Ready, set, school?" Miley's mom asked, tickling Miley in her side.

"Never ever!" Miley protested, but she was laughing.

"Let's do this!" JoJo gathered up her things, stuffing the sparkly birthday planner and glitter pens into her rainbow-patterned tote.

"Miley, let's get the whole crew together after school this week to go over and send out invitations and stuff. Maybe at Grace's place. Her mom has the best snacks, and they just got a giant trampoline for their backyard."

"Sounds perfect," Miley said.

"Buckle up, ladies," Miley's mom reminded them as the girls slid into the back of her car. "First stop—school. And JoJo, am I dropping you back at your house after this, or at the studio?"

"Home! Mom and I are doing school before we head over to the studio for a recording session," JoJo explained. "Plus, I miss Bow-Bow." JoJo liked to bring her cuddly little teacup Yorkie with her everywhere, but dogs were not allowed in doughnut shops—which was practically a crime against dogs, if you asked JoJo.

Miley's mom gave the girls a thumbs-up in the mirror. "How did the planning go?" she wanted to know.

"It went great, Mom," said Miley. "I definitely want to do it at an ice-skating rink, and my friends are handling the decorations. Except Jacob can't do the cake, so you'll have to handle that."

Her mom nodded. "On it. I think I can handle a cake and maybe even a couple of pizzas too," she said, pulling off the freeway and onto the road to Miley's school. "JoJo, would you like to join us on Saturday to scout ice-skating venues? I did a little research of my own while you two were planning," she explained. "There's a perfect rink about twenty minutes from our neighborhood that allows Saturday rentals, and it even has a disco ball, playlist hookup for our phones, and an adjoining party room for snacks. I

14

want us to go see it in person this weekend. You girls could even test it out, if you want." She smiled into the rearview mirror.

"Mom. You. Are. Amazing," said Miley.

"I sure am," her mom acknowledged. "But also—my baby only turns ten once!"

"Are you tearing up?" JoJo asked, catching Miley's mom's eye in the mirror. "Awww." She giggled. "Moms are so cute."

"This mom is not ready for a tweenager," Mrs. McKenna replied, pulling into the drop-off area of Miley's school.

"Don't worry, Mom," Miley said, unbuckling her seat belt. "We've got a few good years ahead of us yet." She leaned over to give JoJo a squeeze. "You are my favorite friend," she told her.

"You are," said JoJo, hugging her back. Then Miley climbed out of the car, leaned through her mom's window to give her a quick kiss on the cheek, and then dashed through the school's main entrance to find the rest of their friends.

It had been a great morning already, but JoJo couldn't *wait* to get home—she had some birthday surprises for Miley up her sleeve that needed tending to. "Thanks for the lift, Mrs. McKenna," she said, when Miley's mom pulled into her driveway a few minutes later. "See you on Saturday!" Miley's mom waved, and then JoJo was off to do what she did best.

CHAPTER 2

A few days later, JoJo was curled up on an extra-large beanbag chair in Grace's rec room. Kyra was sprawled out on the carpet, fiddling with a fashion app on her iPad. Jacob was busy whipping up some treats in the kitchen—he was in ultra–taste test mode, trying every recipe under the sun for his Junior Pastry Chef contest—and no one was about to complain about that! Miley was nodding her head to the beat of whatever was playing on her headset, moving her body in time to the rhythm. Even BowBow had tagged along! She and Grace's pet corgi, Georgie, were tussling over a squirrel-shaped toy, each grabbing one end and play-growling. The two dogs were best friends, but it was a love-hate relationship when it came to sharing. As for Grace, well . . . Grace was seated at a round white table, biting her lip intently as she worked with stacks of stickers, paper of varying colors, printed photos of Miley, and— duh—glitter glue.

"Jacob! When are those brownies gonna be ready?" JoJo called out. "Some of us are hungry." BowBow barked in acknowledgment, and Miley pulled off her headphones.

"Brownies? Did I hear the word 'brownies'?" Miley asked.

"Oh my gosh," Jacob called back, pretending to be angry. "What am I, your personal chef?"

"Pretty much," Miley said. The girls dissolved in laughter. Jacob pretended to be put out when his friends asked for tastes of his delicious baked confections, but JoJo knew he actually loved the attention, and he loved sharing his favorite pastime with the rest of the Siwanatorz. Siwanatorz were people who made a vow to be kind to everyone. It was a term JoJo had come up with, and it had stuck.

Jacob emerged from the kitchen a minute later with a tray of double-decker, caramel-stuffed, ooey-gooey brownies. Kyra tossed her iPad onto the carpet next to her and leapt to her feet, skipping across the rec room to snatch the first brownie.

"Mmmm, still warm!" she mumbled around her bite, giving her long glossy hair a shake. Her purple and teal streaks—a new look that JoJo fully supported—glimmered against the light of the early-evening sun.

"How good, on a scale of one to redonkulus?" Jacob wanted to know.

"Quadruple infinity redonkulus times a thousand," Kyra said after she finished swallowing.

"Grace? You want one?" JoJo took a brownie for herself, licking a dribble of caramel from her palm, and handed another one to Miley in a napkin.

"Can't! Working," she said, pressing a cut-out heart to the paper in front of her.

"Grace, you aren't seriously making thirty invitations by hand?" JoJo wanted to know. "That will take you forever!"

"No way," Grace said, shaking her head to reveal a smattering of freckles underneath her mane of wavy red hair. "This is just the template. Once I perfect it, I'm going to scan it onto my computer and maybe even add a few more graphics. Then we can email it out to all of Miley's guests!"

"It's looking so, so good," Kyra said. "Oh my gosh. Miley! Grace did a whole collage timeline of important events that happened throughout your first decade. This is so cool."

"Shh," I want to be surprised," Miley said, smiling up from her cross-legged perch atop a green velvet ottoman. "Don't tell me anything else."

"I'll just tell you you're going to love it," JoJo said. Jacob nodded appreciatively at Grace's dazzling design, then absently wandered back toward the kitchen, mumbling something to himself about "sugar doilies."

"And you're also going to love what I've mocked up for our matching shirts," Kyra said, pulling out her iPad. "I do want your input on these, Miley. I want to make sure they're comfortable for skating and glittery enough for your theme."

"Sure!" Miley hopped off the ottoman and joined the others on the sofa. "Wow," she gasped, when Kyra's designs flickered across the screen. "I knew you were into fashion, but, Kyra, these are incredible." Kyra beamed, and JoJo leaned over her shoulder to see better. Miley was right—Kyra's designs were objectively amazing. Her friends were all so talented. It made JoJo's heart swell with pride.

"I was thinking we could do long-sleeve shirts, since it'll be cold in the rink. But then it occurred to me—why not go all out? When you mentioned the skating rink, I started looking up figure-skating costumes. They're gorgeous! Wouldn't it be fun if the four of us had sparkly costumes, personalized with your birthday hashtag? What's it going to be, by the way?"

"I suggested #MileyStone, but Miley didn't like it," JoJo said.

Miley blushed. "I didn't say that, JoJo!"

"It's okay. It's bad. Like, really bad. I'm girl enough to admit it," said JoJo, scooping up BowBow from where she was snoozing with Georgie.

"What about #MagnificentMiley?" Jacob shouted from the other room. "You know, like the Magnificent Mile in Chicago!"

"Hmmm." Miley pondered. "Maybe. Except I've never been to Chicago."

Grace shrugged. "Does it matter?"

"Let's keep thinking," JoJo suggested. "So we know we're doing personalized costumes— ohhh I love that leotard-skirt combo!" The design on Kyra's screen was gorgeous. JoJo couldn't wait to wear it—plus a giant bow, of course.

"Thanks," Kyra said happily. "And for Jacob, I figure this way cool bomber will do." She pulled up an illustration of a bomber jacket with sparkly details to match their leotards.

"That's the coolest of all," JoJo said. "I want that one! I can't decide!"

"Oh my gosh," Miley said. "This reminds me. Can I show you guys what I got in the mail today from my grandparents? I brought them over just so you could see." She rushed to the front hall without waiting for their reply. When she returned, she was cradling a pair of the most beautiful, rainbow-sparkly ice skates JoJo had ever seen.

"They're an early birthday present," Miley explained. "They will go perfectly with our skating outfits!"

"So it's a go, then," JoJo confirmed, just as Jacob brought out a platter of meringue cookies in green, blue, and purple, then waited eagerly for the group to test them.

"It's a go," confirmed Miley. "My mom called the rink and it's available for rental. We just have to take a quick peek on Saturday, and then we're all set for the party!"

"Should we hold off on sending the invites until the rink is locked down?" Grace wanted to know.

"Nah," Miley said. "I can't see myself changing my mind. I haven't been this excited for a birthday party in a decade!"

"Kiddos, time for dinner!" Grace's mom poked her head around the entrance to the living room. "Jacob's been using the kitchen all night, so I ordered egg rolls and fried rice from the Chinese takeout place you all love."

The group cheered. "I am not hungry in the slightest," JoJo confided in Miley. "Not after all those treats Jacob made. But I could go for some chill time for sure. Planning is hard!"

"Yeah—we deserve a reward for our hard work," Grace piped in. "I have to say, I'm feeling good about these invites. They're going to be a masterpiece."

"My ice-skating party is going to be perfect," Miley said. "I can't imagine a better way to turn ten."

JoJo gave her friend a giant hug. Everything was in place for Miley's birthday to be the best party yet. So why did JoJo have a twinge of worry that she couldn't shake?

She pushed away the thought and broke off a teeny-tiny piece of veggie egg roll for Bow-Bow, who was sniffing at her feet. She was silly to worry. What could go wrong when all her favorite people were on the job?

CHAPTER 3

Toot, toot!

BowBow leapt out of her dog bed and spun happy circles in the Siwas' living room when Miley's mom honked the horn for JoJo. It was finally Saturday, one week before Miley's party, and the day they were going to check out the skating rink!

"BowBow, you can't ice-skate," JoJo teased, lifting the pup to her chest and nuzzling

BowBow's fur. JoJo always thought BowBow smelled like tortilla chips, and today was no exception. BowBow licked JoJo's cheek in reply.

"Better get moving," JoJo's mom called from the other room, where she was busy bedazzling a pair of sneakers. "Don't keep Mrs. McKenna waiting!"

"Okay, okay," JoJo said, placing BowBow back on the ground so she could pull on her own bedazzled high-tops. "Bye, Mom! I love you."

"Love you too," her mom replied. "Have fun!"

Twenty minutes later, JoJo, Miley, and Miley's mom pulled into a vast parking lot, jammed with cars. "My," said Mrs. McKenna. "This place is hopping! I had no idea ice skating was so popular in Southern California."

"I didn't even know ice skating *existed* in Southern California!" exclaimed Miley.

"I bet a lot of people do it competitively," JoJo chimed in. "Like, pre-Olympics, even."

"Maybe so," Mrs. McKenna agreed. "In any case, we're here to *par-tay*." JoJo giggled, and Miley rolled her eyes. She usually rolled her eyes at her mom's jokes, but JoJo knew she not-so-secretly thought her mom was the coolest. The three unbuckled their belts, slid out the car, and crossed the parking lot to the indoor rink.

"This place is *awesome*," JoJo exclaimed. Everywhere she looked, there were mirrored disco balls hanging from the lobby's ceiling. Dance music was blasting from overhead speakers, and she spotted a concession stand a few feet away, boasting cotton candy, nachos, pizza, and Swedish Fish. A neon sign positioned over the long counter along the far wall read SKATE RENTAL. The skates up for grabs were a variety of colors and metallic fabrics. JoJo loved everything about the rink. And, from the size of Miley's smile, she thought her best friend felt the same way.

Mrs. McKenna approached the check-in counter.

"I spoke with a Katie Lewis," she informed the woman who was checking people in and handing them their skates.

"I'm Katie Lewis," the woman said, beaming. "Are you perhaps Mrs. McKenna? And you're the birthday girl?" She leaned over the counter to take a look at Miley, who gave her a big grin. Miley's smile was a mirror of her mother's, and their long dark hair shook in tandem as they nodded their agreement.

"And this is my best friend, JoJo Siwa," Miley informed Katie Lewis, beaming proudly.

"JoJo Siwa! My, my. I knew you looked familiar. My daughters are gaga for you. I should have known it was you from your adorable bow," said Katie. "Great to have you here. Now, ladies, could you give me one minute to wrap up back here? I want to get someone to cover for me so I can take you on a tour of the rink. Meanwhile, come on back here and pick out skates in your size."

Miley squealed and beelined right for a pair of ultra-glittery, teal-and-pink skates.

"Miley, those look way too big," whispered JoJo. "You'd better get skates that fit."

"Oh pshaw," said Miley, with a flick of her wrist. "It's this pair or bust."

"I don't know . . ." said JoJo, doubtfully.

"JoJo, please. I really want to wear these ones. I'll be careful."

The skates *were* incredible. Maybe even prettier than the ones Miley's grandparents had sent! Those ones were set to debut the night of Miley's birthday, but for now, JoJo understood why Miley wanted to try out the glitteriest shoes in the rink. JoJo herself picked a blue pleather high-top pair. *So cool,* she thought to herself, tugging them on.

Once they had their skates tied, the group—including Mrs. McKenna and Katie— headed for the rink, Miley's and JoJo's blades compressing the rubber surface covering the facility's interior. JoJo ran as fast as she could in her skate-clad feet. She couldn't wait to get to the ice!

"Whoa, whoa," cautioned Katie. "Have you ever skated before? First rule of thumb: You *will* fall, so take it easy out there."

JoJo and Miley looked at one another and laughed. Katie clearly didn't know that they were professionals—she had a dancer and a dancer-choreographer on her hands!

Katie shook her head. "I'm heading back to my desk now, but give me a shout if you need anything," she told them. "And remember: Be careful!" The girls nodded back at her to show they'd try their very best to behave.

"Behave," however, wasn't in Miley's vocabulary—JoJo knew this from experience. Miley was a force of nature. Even before JoJo connected with the ice, Miley was zipping off to the beat of her favorite pop music. JoJo shook her head at her strong-willed friend and put one foot in front of the other, until she slid into an easy glide.

"This is so fun!" she shouted to Miley, who was lapping her.

"This is the best!" said Miley, who did a twirl, nearly colliding with another skater. Then she shimmied her butt in the style of a

34

dance she'd choreographed to the song that was playing. "This is going to be so fun when we have our Kyra-designed outfits on," she said as JoJo caught up to her. She attempted a mini-jump, and JoJo sucked in a breath, seeing her ankle wobble in its skate on landing. But Miley recovered her balance and seemed unfazed.

"Just imagine this with all our friends and sparkly decorations and a playlist we make ourselves," Miley enthused. "We can do all our favorite dances!" JoJo didn't disagree, but Miley was speeding up; something about it made JoJo nervous. JoJo was super coordinated herself, but even she was a little shaky on her skates, and hers were the right size!

Her friend whizzed past little kids with their parents; smoochy adults holding hands; and some really talented ice-gymnast types who looked like they were maybe in training.

"Watch it," one older boy told Miley when her extended leg almost hit him in the stomach.

"Miley, take it easy, honey!" shouted Miley's mom from the bleachers. "The point is to have fun!"

Miley *was* having fun. She was whizzing through the crowds, bobbing her head to the beat. Then JoJo sucked in a breath. Miley's favorite song *ever* had come on.

It was JoJo's "High Top Shoes."

Miley *loved* that song. She had choreographed a routine for it for JoJo to perform on tour. And now she was doing all the things a person should do in high-top shoes . . . but *not* in ice skates. Miley was jumping and even twirling midair, as though she'd been on skates for years.

"Miley!" Mrs. McKenna's voice had a note of worry in it now. JoJo could see her

36

friend getting caught up in the choreography. She looked good. Actually, she looked *great*. But JoJo knew from experience that you didn't get anything perfect the first time around.

JoJo decided to try to get Miley to bring it down a notch. She skated up to her friend and was just reaching out to grab her hand when—mid-twirl—Miley face-planted on the ice.

"Miley!" JoJo shouted. Miley was resting on her knees, but her left ankle was folded under her, and tears were forming in the corners of her eyes.

"Are you okay?" JoJo was breathless. She crouched down next to her friend, who was wincing and gripping her ankle. "Can you stand up?" Miley shook her head and bit her lip hard. Her cheeks were pale, and her ankle was bent at a funny angle.

"I'm getting help," JoJo told her. "Stay right there."

JoJo's heart was beating like crazy—faster than the tempo of the music, even—as she skated back toward the bleachers where they'd left Miley's mom. But Miley's mom was already on her feet and dashing onto the ice in her sneakers, slipping and sliding the whole way. By then, Miley was beginning to cry openly—and Miley was the toughest girl JoJo knew. JoJo pulled her own skates off, slid on her sneakers, and dashed to the front desk, where she told Katie what happened.

"Sweetheart," Miley's mom was saying when the two rejoined them. "Can you stand?" She wrapped her arm around Miley, who shifted her weight onto her right side and tried to rise up. When she tried to put weight on her left leg, though, she promptly collapsed.

"Let's at least unlace your skates, honey," Mrs. McKenna said, reaching for the laces. Katie placed a hand on Miley's mom's wrist.

"I wouldn't do that," Katie said. "I've seen a lot of injuries on the ice, and sometimes removing the skates can make it worse by jogging the wound. Better to leave them on and let the doctor handle it."

"I'll bring them back," Miley's mom promised.

"Don't worry about it—you can keep them," said Katie. "Let's just get this girl patched up."

"I'll have to lift her." Miley's mom scooped Miley in her arms as if Miley was a baby again, cradling her against her chest. "Hold the doors, JoJo." JoJo dashed to the rink's exit and held open the doors as Mrs. McKenna walked through, holding Miley. Katie followed with their bags. JoJo's heart sped up at the sight of Miley wincing and biting her bottom lip.

"Honey, I'm going to take Miley to the hospital," Mrs. McKenna told JoJo. "Why don't you text your mom and have her meet us there? I think Miley and I might be a while."

JoJo hopped into the front seat while Mrs. McKenna placed Miley in the back—injured leg propped up on the bench—and buckled her in. She shot off a quick text to her mom, asking her to pick her up from the hospital. "*Bring Miley the BowBow stuffed animal,*" she added—Miley could use a pick-me-up. JoJo snuck glances at her friend in the back seat. Miley wasn't crying anymore, but her face was unnaturally pale. JoJo reached back and squeezed her hand tight.

When they pulled into the hospital, JoJo's mom was already waiting for them out front with a couple of nurses, a wheelchair, and—of course—a BowBow stuffed animal for Miley to cuddle.

"I've never ridden in a wheelchair before," Miley said, trying for a smile as the nurses placed her in the chair.

"That's my girl," Mrs. McKenna said. Then she turned to JoJo and her mom. "We'll call you afterward to let you know how things go."

"I want to stay," JoJo said. "Mom, can we stay?"

"Of course, if you want," JoJo's mom said. "Best friends stick together."

CHAPTER 4

It was nearly four hours later when the nurse wheeled Miley back out, her left leg bundled to the knee in a cast. Miley's mom had a pair of crutches tucked under her arm. JoJo's heart sank, but she pasted on a bright smile.

"Miley has a hairline fracture in her ankle," Mrs. McKenna explained. "She'll be okay in six to eight weeks, but unfortunately there'll be no ice-skating next weekend." Miley frowned, her eyes downcast. JoJo hugged her friend,

handing her a bunch of balloons she'd purchased at the hospital gift shop, along with
the toy BowBow.

"We'll think of an even better party, Miley!"
JoJo exclaimed. "And we'll save skating for
another time."

"You're a good friend, JoJo," Miley's mom
told her. JoJo bit her lip. In addition to playing
around on her mom's iPad, she had done a
lot of thinking while Miley was getting X-rays
and fitted for a cast. Now that Miley's skates
were gone, she figured it was time to 'fess up.

"I would have been a better friend if I
hadn't let you wear skates that didn't fit," JoJo
said in one breath.

"It was my decision," Miley told her. "You
let me know you didn't think it was a good
idea. But I was the one who made a bad
choice. You're the *best* friend, JoJo!"

"Awww," JoJo said, leaning in for a hug.

43

"Well. I'll have to get the background on that later," JoJo's mom said, giving JoJo a significant look. "But it sounds like today was a learning experience for everyone. I say let's dial back on the learning for a sec. I don't know about you guys, but I could use a little ice cream after all that hospital."

"Yay!" shouted Miley. "That's *exactly* what I need." She hoisted herself from her wheelchair and reached for the crutches. "Watch my moves, JoJo!" Then she was off toward the car, using the crutches to do a little swing-plus-skipping move that JoJo could swear was a move straight out of a Beyoncé video. JoJo laughed, and Miley's mom face-palmed.

"This girl," Miley's mom confided to JoJo's mom, "is going to give me a run for my money."

"Did someone say 'run'?" Miley piped up from down the block. "Ready . . . set . . ."

"Miley, no!"

44

"What are we going to do?" Jacob asked, chewing forlornly on a homemade chocolate biscotti. "Miley had her heart set on that ice-skating party!"

"And the invitations already went out," Grace reminded them. "We'll have to email everyone to cancel."

"What a bummer," said Kyra. "Poor Miley!"

JoJo had called an emergency meeting of her fellow Siwanatorz—minus Miley—the following afternoon. They had serious business to discuss: Miley was turning ten in less than a week, and her party had been completely derailed. Rumor had it Miley's mom was planning to make her a nice dinner with all her favorite foods at home for her birthday. Technically it wasn't a rumor (JoJo just liked the phrase "rumor had it"). It was fact—because JoJo was invited. It was a sweet idea, but . . . ten only came once! JoJo couldn't let

45

her BFF settle for less than the literal party of the decade.

"It is a huge bummer," JoJo said, pulling BowBow into her lap for a cuddle. The group was in JoJo's room in various states of recline. "But I've done a lot of thinking, and I bet we can still pull off the party Miley wanted."

"JoJo, what do you mean? Miley's on crutches."

"Grace, think big," JoJo explained. "We'll bring the party to Miley! As long as Mrs. McKenna can host, we can use all our same decorations. We can email everyone a new location but keep the time the same. What's the next best party to an ice-skating party?"

"A surprise party!" Grace shouted, just as Kyra yelled, "A slumber party!"

"Fair points," Jacob agreed. "Those are definitely the best kinds of parties."

"So we'll combine them into a double-whammy, double-digit, sparkle-themed extravaganza," JoJo decided, clapping her hands. "Great meeting, Siwanatorz. Let's get to work. We have less than one week to plan."

After getting permission from her mom, JoJo called Miley's mom and pitched the Siwanatorz's Double-Whammy, Double-Digit, Sparkle-Themed Soiree.

"I swear, you kids are creative," Miley's mom laughed. "Of *course* you can have a party here! I'll leave the key under the big potted fern on our front stoop. Miley has a follow-up appointment with the doctor at noon on Saturday, so you can slip in then to set up. And I'll take Miley for a birthday lunch afterward to buy you a little more time."

"That sounds so great, Mrs. McKenna," JoJo exclaimed. "I think if we pull this off, our party will be even better than the original!"

"I have a few surprises up my sleeve too." Through the phone, JoJo could sense Mrs. McKenna smiling. JoJo didn't pry—after all, what fun would it be if she knew everything?

As soon as JoJo hung up the phone, she sent a group text to Grace, Kyra, and Jacob: *It's a go—send out the updated evite!*

Grace texted back the unicorn emoji plus the kissy cat face emoji. (The emoji-inventors hadn't made a caticorn yet.) Jacob sent back the chef emoji with the tiny spatula. Kyra sent back the manicure emoji. All of it was code for *Siwanatorz: Let's do this.*

As soon as Grace sent out the new evite, RSVPs started pouring in.

"Everyone is obsessed with our new party concept," JoJo informed Kyra on FaceTime. "Even though we're keeping the slumber party small." Miley's mom hadn't been prepared to host thirty kids all night, but she said Kyra, Grace, and JoJo were welcome to stay over. "Grace made sure to note that everyone should come wearing sparkles—so now it's not just the décor that'll be sparkly, it's the guests too!"

"Who wouldn't be obsessed with that?" asked Kyra. "By the way, I'm still designing our outfits. I'm in the midst of a serious sequin craze. You wouldn't believe the shiny purple ones I found. They look blue-green in a certain light. Talk about cutting-edge fashion."

"Hold that thought," JoJo said. "You just reminded me. Miley is obsessed with some old movie about figure skating that her mom got her into. What if we set it up on the projector during the slumber party? That way she can still feel like skating's a part of the night."

"Genius," Kyra agreed. "And by the way, I decided to go with bomber jackets for all of our coordinating sparkly outfits, not just Jacob's. I figured the whole leotard look might just remind Miley of what she's missing . . . and not in a good way."

"Yeah, we can't attend Miley's party wearing skating costumes. I mean we *can*," JoJo corrected herself. "But I agree that bombers are the way to go. Plus then Jacob won't feel left out!"

"Exactly. He's already missing the slumber party," Kyra mentioned. "I think he's a little bummed."

"Well. He has to wake up at 5 a.m. the day after the party to travel to the California Junior Pastry Chef contest. So actually, he probably won't feel left out at all. He'll just be thinking about the contest."

"He's been practice-baking for weeks," said Kyra. "I never thought I'd say these words, but

I might need a break from sugar for a while. If I have to taste-test one more madeleine . . ."

"Give it twenty-four hours," JoJo laughed. "You'll be just fine."

"He's made, like, *thousands* of pastries," Kyra marveled. "I bet he has a good shot at winning. I just wish we could watch it on TV."

"One day, when he's super famous, we will," JoJo assured her friend. "But for now, that's why we have FaceTime!"

"Oh em gee," Kyra said, a note of anxiety in her voice. "He *is* going to be super famous someday. I have to start designing outfits for our red carpet debuts right now!"

JoJo laughed. Kyra was always one design ahead of the game.

CHAPTER 5

A week filled with studio recording time and voice lessons and school and party prepping finally gave way to Saturday: Miley's birthday. JoJo woke up at 8 a.m.—the crack of dawn for her!—and texted Miley right away.

Hi, bday girl!!! Happy birthday! I can't wait to have dinner with you tonight! <3

In part because of how busy she'd been all week, JoJo hadn't seen Miley even once since her friend's accident. The other part was because JoJo couldn't keep a secret from Miley—one suspicious smirk would give the whole plan away! So when Miley requested to FaceTime, JoJo ignored the call, then fired off a quick text:

Gtg help my mom with some stuff! See ya later!

The message screen flashed with three dots—Miley was typing. Then she stopped. No message came through.

Weird. JoJo figured Miley must have gotten distracted. She fired off a quick heart emoji, pulled on her favorite sequined joggers and matching hoodie, and ran downstairs. She did have to help her mom with some stuff— they were creating Miley's surprise birthday banner! And JoJo had thought of a couple of hashtag options: #MileyOnTheMend and #MTurns10. She shared them with Grace, Jacob, and Kyra in a quick text with a bunch of smiley face emojis. JoJo's friends loved to make fun of her hashtags—they thought they were cheesy. But JoJo loved her hashtags, so she texted them around whenever they came to mind. Peace out, haterz!

By the time JoJo and her mom finished the banner, it was the biggest, sparkliest, most beautiful banner JoJo had ever seen! It read, "Surprise, Miley!" and featured blow-up cut-out photos of Miley making silly faces, to match Grace's evite. At the last second, JoJo had left the hashtags off because the vote was split. Life was hard. It was nearly time for Miley and her mom to leave for the doctor.

Operation slumber party sparkles: green light? She texted Mrs. McKenna.

Green light! Mrs. McKenna typed back. *We're out the door in 5. Cake delivery 1 hr.*

JoJo also sent a text to Miley, who'd been conspicuously quiet all morning—probably distracted by family birthday celebrating, or sleeping in, or, JoJo figured, painting her nails something sparkly.

Good luck at your doctor's appt!!!!! JoJo typed. Oops—I mean break a leg! Lolol

She giggled. Miley would totally send back the eyeroll emoji. JoJo pocketed her phone. "Ready, Mom," she called out. The two loaded the car with the sparkly banner, homemade disco balls, and JoJo's wrapped gift for Miley. Then they swung by Grace's, Kyra's, and Jacob's houses. When the whole crew was assembled, they went on to Miley's.

"I'll wait in the car until I'm sure you got in," Mrs. Siwa told the kids, who gathered armfuls of supplies and headed up Miley's driveway. When they reached the door to Miley's house, JoJo scooted aside the terra-cotta planter that held the plant Miley called a "welcome fern." Sure enough, the key was just underneath.

"Sweet," Jacob said. "Breaking in! I feel so criminal."

Grace elbowed him. "Jacob! We are *not* breaking in. We are using a key that we were given permission to use."

"Let me have my fun," Jacob said, just as JoJo felt the key click into place and the lock give way. JoJo waved to her mom, who waved back from the car. And then the four Siwana-torz were free to plan the ultimate party.

J oJo was standing on a barstool taping the banner to the wall when Kyra ran in, her face flushed. "JoJo!" she shouted. "Pull that down *now*. They're back!"

"What do you mean they're back?" JoJo asked. "Who's back? My mom?"

"No!" shouted Grace from her perch in the living room. Her voice was high-pitched and nervous sounding. "It's Miley and her mom!

The car is in the driveway! Miley's getting out! They're both coming in! Hurry!"

"What the . . . ?" JoJo leapt into action, pulling the banner back down. They'd only been there for fifteen minutes—why had Miley and her mom returned? "Hide, every-one, quick!" JoJo shouted. "Basement! Miley hates the basement!" But there was no time. The front doorknob was already begin-ning to turn. JoJo darted for the downstairs bathroom. Jacob looked like he was head-ing toward the kitchen, naturally. She didn't have time to keep track of the others. JoJo stepped into the shower and tugged the cur-tain closed behind her. She heard Miley enter the foyer.

"I don't know why you insisted on coming in with me, sweetie," Mrs. McKenna was say-ing, her voice laced with worry. "You should be staying off your ankle."

"Mom. You know you'd never find my cell phone yourself. It'd be like a needle in a haystack."

So they came back for her phone, JoJo realized. She desperately hoped it wasn't in the bathroom.

"I don't want to miss any birthday messages, since I won't be seeing anyone today. Well, anyone except JoJo," Miley continued, sounding sad.

"We'll throw a big party once you're up and running again." Mrs. McKenna's voice was thick with cheer. "We're going to be late for your appointment, Miley. If you don't find it in two minutes, you're going to have to leave it behind."

Miley's footsteps—which were easy to identify because of the thump of the crutches—passed alarmingly close to the bathroom. JoJo held her breath. Where was everyone else hiding? Would they blow their cover? Shoot. Miley was definitely heading toward the kitchen.

JoJo heard some cabinets open and close. Why would Miley's phone be in the cabinetry?! JoJo shook her head. Miley was so weird sometimes. She held her breath that Jacob wasn't camped out in the pantry.

Then she heard the rustle of the trash can being pulled out from under the sink.

"Aha!" Miley shouted. "I found it! I accidentally threw it away!"

"Miley . . . oh my goodness," said Mrs. McKenna. "Well. At least you found it. Now let's get going."

"Hold on, I'm just checking my messages," Miley said. JoJo felt like her heart was about to explode out of her chest. At any minute, Miley could find one of them.

"Oh," Miley said, forlorn.

"What is it?" Mrs. McKenna moved past the hallway bathroom and, as far as JoJo could tell, toward the kitchen to join Miley. Mrs. McKenna's footsteps were smoother and harder to track. "Miley! Honey, why are you crying?"

"I don't have any more messages from JoJo," Miley explained. "And she ignored my FaceTime today. And I haven't seen her all week. I just feel like . . . Where is she? She should be here with me when I'm lonely and she knows my ankle hurts." JoJo sucked in a breath. But she'd texted Miley earlier! And Miley hadn't responded! Should she have texted again?

"I'm sure JoJo is thinking about you," JoJo heard Mrs. McKenna tell Miley. "She probably has good reasons for being busy."

"I guess," said Miley. JoJo felt a pang. It didn't occur to her that the whole time JoJo was avoiding Miley to hide the surprise, Miley might have *noticed* JoJo avoiding Miley and taken it the wrong way. It took everything she had not to burst out of the bathroom and 'fess up to her friend.

"Let's go, honey," Mrs. McKenna said gently. "You'll see JoJo later on. I have the feeling it'll all work out."

Miley mumbled something JoJo couldn't make out, then the two headed back toward the front door, Miley's thumping steps followed by her mom's lighter ones. Only after JoJo heard the car pull out of the driveway did she let out a big sigh and emerge from the bathroom.

"Did you guys hear that?" she asked Grace, Kyra, and Jacob.

"Yeah," Grace said. "But don't worry, JoJo. She'll understand when she sees our amazing party." JoJo hoped Grace was right. The

61

party was due to start in four hours. Four hours was a long time to accidentally hurt your best friend. JoJo reached for her phone. When she opened her text window, she gasped. She'd forgotten to hit "send" after she wrote her last message to Miley! No wonder she was hurt.

She typed out another quick text to Miley: *Can't wait to see you boo J*

After double-checking that she hit "send" this time, she put down her phone, picked up the discarded banner, and hoped for the best.

CHAPTER 6

JoJo felt a trickle of sweat slide down her back. She and her friends had covered the entire bottom level of the house with streamers of all colors, glitter banners, and unicorn glitter-bomb piñatas stuffed with Miley's favorite candy. They even had one giant piñata shaped like a giant, glittery ice skate. They had asked Miley's dad, who'd come home shortly after Miley and her mom left, to set up the projector outside with the figure-skating movie and all its sequels. They'd put all the snacks Miley's mom had purchased in bowls on the dining room table, underneath a gold-sequined tablecloth Grace and Kyra had teamed up to make—it was covered in patches shaped like bows, rainbows, hearts, skates, cupcakes, and music notes.

Party prepping was hard work!

JoJo was just settling onto the living room sofa, eager for a break, when the doorbell rang.

"I'll get it," called Mr. McKenna. "It's probably the cake."

Miley's mom had ordered a three-tier, custom cake shaped like a pair of ice skates, with a big number ten shaped out of cake and leaning in front of it. Jacob had been dying to take a look at it all morning.

"Can you imagine the quality of fondant they must have used?" he was saying, as Mr. McKenna hauled the giant box inside. "Oh my gosh. Do you think they used edible glitter?"

"A cake is hardly even a cake without edible glitter these days," commented Kyra from the kitchen, where she was filling a glass of water.

"You kids are older than your years," Mr. McKenna laughed. "When I was a kid, my mom baked me cakes from a box!"

"Mmm, funfetti," Grace mentioned. "Boxed cakes still hold up, Mr. McKenna." He smiled at her around the side of the cake—but his face was hardly visible and he was clearly struggling to balance the giant confection. "I'll just put it over here," he said, angling his body toward the dining room. "Don't want to have to move it again."

"Mr. McKenna! No!" chorused JoJo and Grace. What Mr. McKenna couldn't see was that Kyra was in the process of creating a faux-rink between the foyer and the dining room, complete with a homemade Slip 'N Slide that guests could "skate" on in their socks. The Slip 'N Slide was doused in slippery floor polish!

It was too late. Mr. McKenna's socked feet slid. His hands faltered. The cake jiggled, threatening to topple. The kids rushed toward it, but in their rushing, they forgot they too would slide . . . directly into Mr. McKenna.

The cake flew from his hands and landed with a crash on the wooden floorboards. The box popped apart, and bits of cake flew everywhere. It was horrible and beautiful all at once.

"Well," JoJo said cautiously. "It's a good thing BowBow isn't here. She'd gobble it up in no time, then get sick."

"Mrs. McKenna is not going to be happy about this," Mr. McKenna commented with a frown.

"It looks like the '10' is salvageable," Jacob commented, peering at the mess. "It's a little cracked, but that fondant sure held! I think I can patch it up."

"Jacob, you have to practice for your contest tomorrow," Grace reminded him. "It's going to take a lot of time to patch that cake."

"And even so, the cake isn't enough to go around," Mr. McKenna commented. "It's okay, Jacob. We'll figure something else out."

"No. Way," Jacob insisted. "The skate is worthless for sure, but I'll fix the '10'—this is my thing! And"—His eyes lit up—"I have just the solution for the rest of the treats!"

"You do?" Kyra was skeptical. Jacob's "solutions" usually wound up being hours-long baking sprees.

"Totally," Jacob said. "I've been baking hundreds of cookies for the past few weeks, and they're all stored in a spare freezer in my parents' basement. We can just thaw them and make a nice display around the ten!"

"Genius," Grace assured him, smiling kindly.

"Hmm, that may not be a bad idea," Mr. McKenna said thoughtfully. "You know, my mother's family is Italian, and growing up we always had a cookie table tradition at weddings. There were dozens of different kinds of cookies, and everyone took a box home with them. That might be a nice touch. As long as you don't mind donating your cookies, Jacob."

"Not at all," Jacob said. "But I'll need to run back down the block to my house to get them, and to get the fixin's for the cake."

"Okay, Grandpa," Kyra teased. "Get the fixin's."

Jacob stuck out his tongue. "No triple chocolate petit fours for you!"

"Are you sure you want to deal with all that?" JoJo was a little nervous. If Jacob wasn't able to do it, his confidence might be shaken before his competition. She really wanted Jacob to go into the baking contest with a strong mindset.

"I've got this, JoJo," Jacob said. "Trust me."

"We've got two hours until they're back," she warned.

"It'll be good training for the timed portions of the contest. Besides, what are you always saying?"

"Siwanatorz believe in each other!" Grace pitched in.

"It's true," Kyra added. "Jacob's a whiz.

Let's just treat this like the ultimate test run for the contest!"

"Okay, sounds good to me," JoJo said. "We're doing pretty well on time with the rest of the stuff. Jacob, how can we help?"

"I'll need help lugging the supplies," Jacob explained. "Mr. McKenna, do you have any kind of suitcase or big bucket?"

"I can do you one better," Mr. McKenna said. "We have an old wheelbarrow. Why don't you use that?"

"Perfect," Jacob said. "JoJo, why don't you come help me? Kyra and Grace can stay here and hold down the fort."

"Great—I'm still adding final details to our jackets," Kyra said.

"And I feel like a #MileyOnTheMend poster is in order," Grace said, sneaking a look at JoJo.

"You love my hashtag!" cheered JoJo.

Grace giggled. "I always love them, JoJo," she said. "I just give you a hard time." She winked.

A year ago, Grace had been so shy. JoJo loved that she was comfortable enough being herself to joke around. JoJo threw her arms around her friend.

"We'll be back!" she said. "You two make sure Mr. McKenna doesn't break anything else!"

"Hey!" came a protest from the kitchen, but JoJo and Jacob were already halfway out the door.

"I'm actually kind of glad this happened, in a way," Jacob said, pushing the wheelbarrow with JoJo in it. "Oof! I don't know if I can push you all the way down the block," he huffed. "But anyway, this lets me practice for

71

tomorrow *and* make Miley a cake. It feels like it was meant to be."

"You're the best, you know that?" JoJo said. "Especially when you're chauffeuring my wheelbarrow."

Jacob made a quick feint to the right as if he meant to dump JoJo, then quickly righted the wheelbarrow. JoJo was giggling. "You wouldn't," she said.

"I might." JoJo looked back to see Jacob wiggling his eyebrows. She hopped off and took hold of the wheelbarrow.

"I've got it from here," she said, speeding up on the sidewalk until she hit a jog, the wheelbarrow clattering in front of her. Jacob jogged alongside her, huffing.

"Wait up," he said.

"We don't have a second to lose," JoJo laughed.

The two burst through the front door of

72

Jacob's house, exactly seven houses down and one street over from Miley's.

"My mom and dad are out at a play," Jacob said. "But we can help ourselves to the baking cupboard. I'll text and let them know." He dashed off a few lines on his phone. "Now. We need a lot of ingredients for fondant." He reached in the cupboards and began pulling bags and canisters from the shelves. "This pantry is all mine," he said. "Mom and Dad had it put in when I got serious about baking. We already have all the ingredients here, so we're good."

"There are, like, eight ingredients," JoJo pointed out.

"Sure. Plus some fun special touches," Jacob said. "I'm not just re-creating, I'm re-inventing!"

The two tossed all the ingredients in the wheelbarrow, then grabbed a half dozen

73

ziplock bags stuffed with cookies from the freezer and added them to the pile. They pushed their load back to Miley's place. "I am so down for this," JoJo said. "Miley doesn't even know what she's in for."

"Sometimes the unexpected stuff is the best stuff," Jacob agreed. Then he set to work in the kitchen as JoJo, Kyra, and Grace collectively held their breaths.

CHAPTER 7

Jacob knocked himself out with the cake. Grace knocked herself out with the decorations. Kyra's bomber jackets were, well, *bomb*. They were hanging in the coat closet at the entryway of Miley's house, just waiting for the Siwanatorz to throw them on. And as for JoJo . . . she'd been helping with everything, but she was keeping her own surprise for Miley a secret. Mr. McKenna made himself scarce while the kids made Miley's home as party-worthy as they possibly could.

At 4 p.m., the guests began arriving. JoJo couldn't believe how incredible their outfits were. They'd gone all out! There were sparkly pink flamingo costumes, sparkly headdresses, sparkly knee-length dresses, sparkly joggers and sneakers . . . everything sparkly under the sun!

Everyone filed into Miley's house and helped themselves to cotton candy from a cotton-candy spinner the McKenna's had rented specifically for the occasion. Kyra put on Miley's signature party playlist, and Grace arranged piles of gifts on a table by the front door. JoJo was in the middle of helping Jacob put the finishing touches on the cookie table when she heard a loud "shush" from one of their guests.

"She's here!" cried Grace, running over to JoJo. "Everyone—shhhhh."

The guests went quiet.

The lock in the front door turned.

Mrs. McKenna pushed her way in, holding the door ajar for Miley.

Miley wobbled in on her crutches and . . .

"SURPRISE!" everyone yelled in unison. Miley tottered—Mrs. McKenna reached out to steady her. "Happy birthday, Miley!"

Miley leaned into one crutch and wiped her eyes with her opposite palm. JoJo ran up to her and wrapped her in a hug. "You didn't think I'd let your birthday go by without pulling out all the stops," she said, "did you?"

"JoJo, you put all this together?" Miley's voice was a whisper.

"No. We all did!" Grace, Kyra, and Jacob crowded around Miley. "Wait until you see the surprises we have for you, Miley. You'll be *glad* you couldn't have a skating party, because this new party is so much better!"

"Oh my gosh, Grace, your art is incredible," Miley breathed, looking up at the big, glittery poster that hung on the wall between the foyer and the living room. "JoJo. #MileyOnTheMend? Not bad."

"Okay, but now I'm kind of into #MTurns10," JoJo explained.

"There have been many options," Kyra chimed in. "But my favorite was #MaginificentMiley." She plucked one of the sparkly bombers from the hall closet and presented it to Miley. "That's why I decided to put it on the back of our matching bombers."

"Oh em gee, so cute!" Miley squealed. "You guys really know how to make a girl feel special!"

"Okay but . . . come see this," Miley's mom said. "Your father broke your cake, honey. So look what your friends did!"

The crew walked with Miley to the kitchen.

"No way!" Miley exclaimed. The other guests crowded around her, oohing and aahing. Not only had Jacob fixed the giant frosted number ten—by pasting together a cracked "1"—he'd raised it vertically and rested it against what looked like a cookie mountain. And on top of it all—at the top of the mountain, raising her arms in the air— was a perfect, six-inch-tall likeness of Miley. Miley was staring at it, jaw hanging open. JoJo thought she could see the beginnings of tears welling in her eyes. JoJo had to admit that what Jacob had pulled together was beyond anything she could have imagined. It was all Miley.

Mrs. McKenna lit candles around the base of the cake, illuminating it in all its glory. Just then, JoJo kicked off a round of "Happy Birthday."

"Make a wish," JoJo reminded Miley, and her friend bent over the cake, her father helping steady her on her crutches. Miley blew out all ten candles at once, beaming among spirals of smoke. Then they all dug into Jacob's masterpiece.

Three piñatas later and the McKenna household was *covered* in glitter. "Oh my," Mrs. McKenna said, surveying the living room. "Well that's the sign of a great party!"

"And it isn't over yet," Miley's dad said. "Sweetheart, we have a surprise for you out back."

"And I have a surprise for you too!" chimed JoJo. "But that'll come later."

80

Everyone filed into the backyard through the sliding door in the kitchen. The yard was empty beyond the family's swimming pool, the pool house, and a giant bale of hay.

"Why is there a bale of hay in our backyard?" Miley wanted to know, her forehead wrinkled in an expression of confusion.

"It's for our visitor," her mom said. JoJo, Miley, Kyra, Grace, and Jacob exchanged glances. No one knew what on earth Mrs. McKenna was talking about.

"Let's go check the pool house," Miley's dad told her. "It's a bit of a hike on crutches, but I think you need to see this for yourself." He helped Miley across the concrete path that lead around the pool to the pool house. Once they got there, Miley flung open the door to the guest house. Then JoJo heard a shriek! She looked over at Miley's mom—Mrs. McKenna was giggling, so everything was probably okay. But then what . . . ?

JoJo gasped. Miley emerged from the guest house on her crutches, and just behind her was her dad, holding the lead to what appeared to be . . .

. . . the very cutest miniature pony she had ever seen—in real life *or* on the internet.

The pony only came up to Miley's knee. It had a long mane with a sparkly bow perched jauntily atop its head.

Miley was so happy she burst into tears.

JoJo ran over and threw her arms around her best friend. "Miley! It's what you've always wanted," she said.

"I've wanted a pony so bad, I've had a name picked out for years," Miley admitted. "And this pony is *totally* a Dusty."

"Dusty! So sweet!"

82

"Miley, Dusty is going to be living at the ranch down the street," her dad explained, "where she'll have plenty of land to run around in and a comfortable shed and lots of care. But she can visit us here and you can visit her there anytime you want! One of the ranch hands even came out today with Dusty to give everyone a lesson on care and feeding." Miley's dad motioned in the direction of a woman wearing cowboy boots, who was standing at the edge of the group. JoJo hadn't noticed her earlier. She had brown hair pulled back in a ponytail and a freckled face that looked a little younger than JoJo's mom. She smiled and approached the pony.

"Who wants to learn some grooming techniques?" she asked to a round of cheers from JoJo and her friends. A few minutes later, Miley was seated in a lawn chair and carefully brushing Dusty's forelock, mane, and tail according to the woman—Jane's—instructions. Jane had told everyone to be very gentle with the pony's hair, since it can take years for it to grow back if it's broken.

Jane gave Grace a damp washcloth to wipe Dusty's face. Grace made sure to stay away from Dusty's eyes, as Jane told her to. Finally, Jane let JoJo braid Dusty's hair.

"Dusty is a very special pony," Jane told the group. "We've been waiting for her to find the perfect owner, Miley, and I can see you're a great fit. Look how calm she is with you!" Miley beamed at the praise and patted the horse's nose. In response, Dusty nuzzled her palm.

"I love her so much. Thank you," she told her parents. She reached for her left crutch, which was lying on the lawn beside her, and pulled herself to standing. Then she handed it off to JoJo and leaned on her right side, as she wrapped her left arm around her mom, then angled her head up to give her dad a kiss on the cheek. "This is truly the best birthday ever. I have the sweetest, most thoughtful, most loving family and friends."

"And you thought we forgot all about you!" JoJo exclaimed. "We would never! I heard you when you came back for your phone—we were already here setting up. We had to hide!"

"Oh my gosh!" Miley blushed. "I'm sorry, JoJo. I was really upset about what happened at the skating rink. I should never have doubted you guys. I think sometimes when I get focused on something and want it to happen, I forget to leave room for surprises."

"It's a good life lesson," her mom commented. "Sometimes surprises can be better than the original plan, if you're open to them."

"Okay, okay," JoJo said. "Enough of the life lessons." She grinned up at Miley's parents so they'd know she was teasing. "Now can I *finally* share my surprise?"

"I don't know if I can handle more!" Miley exclaimed.

"Well, you're gonna have to," JoJo said. "You only hit this *Mileystone* once! Get it?" Her friends all groaned, and JoJo laughed. "Okay, so, here's a gift from me and my parents." She handed Miley an envelope and held her breath as Miley slid it open. This was phase 1 of her birthday surprise for Miley.

"No way!" Miley said, grinning at JoJo.

"What is it?" Kyra wanted to know.

"It's ice-skating lessons for me and JoJo, for when I get better," Miley explained. "That's so cool."

"I was a little afraid you wouldn't want to do it anymore, after what happened," JoJo said. "But then I remembered . . . this is Miley we're talking about. *Nothing* gets her down."

"That's right," Miley laughed. "I'm just as obsessed as I was two weeks ago, don't worry."

"Well, I for one am glad you'll be skating with an instructor," said Miley's dad. "Whom you'll have to *listen to*." He gave Miley a look of mock-warning.

"Oh, Dad." Miley rolled her eyes, then pulled him into another hug.

"All right, everyone." Miley's mom addressed the cluster of friends who were crowded around Dusty. "Listen up! Who wants to hear a concert?" Her request was met with cheers—everyone knew she meant JoJo was going to perform, and everyone loved when JoJo put on spontaneous shows just for them.

"I wanna hear 'Boomerang!'" shouted one kid.

"No, JoJo, sing 'High Top Shoes'!" someone else said.

JoJo shook her head. "No way," she replied. "Not today! Today I'm debuting a brand-new song." She turned to Miley. "And I wrote it just for you." She and Miley shared a hug, and then Mr. McKenna helped Grace and Jacob pull out the mini-stage and microphone they'd rigged up that afternoon.

JoJo hopped on the stage and took the mic. Then she belted out a song all about friendship—but more specifically, about her very best friend, Miley, on her tenth birthday. It was the first time anyone was hearing the song . . . and the crowd went wild.

Later, after all the guests had helped themselves to goodie bags full of Jacob's cookies, the crew settled down on the back lawn with a big box of pizza. Miley's dad had set up the projector for their movie marathon. The night was balmy, but just crisp enough that they were all sporting their new sparkly bomber jackets.

"This is henceforth my lucky bomber," Jacob said. "I'm totally wearing it to the contest tomorrow. I wish I didn't have to go soon!"

"You need some real sleep after today," JoJo commented, playing with the bow detailing on the jacket, which Kyra had added just for her. "You really pulled out all the stops, Jacob."

"Any situation like this where I'm really challenged is great training," Jacob assured her. "I loved it. And I probably won't sleep anyway, I'm so excited!"

"Well you *do* need to eat," Grace said. "So here, have another slice of pizza." She pushed the box toward Jacob, and JoJo smiled at her most nurturing friend. A few minutes later, Jacob stood up to go.

"Give me a call if you need a pro to weigh in on truth or dare," he told them.

"We will! And FaceTime us after the contest tomorrow," JoJo replied. Jacob gave them a thumbs-up and walked out the back gate, just as dusk was beginning to fall. The girls were sad to see Jacob go, but the best part of the party was only just beginning.

CHAPTER 8

"**B**efore we start watching the movie, I have a request to make," Grace said shyly. JoJo looked up in surprise from the chair she was lounging on, poolside. Miley's parents had taken Dusty back to the stables for the night, despite *much* begging on Miley's part to let Dusty join the slumber party. Grace was usually the go-with-the-flow type, the last person to express a need, so right now, all the focus turned to her.

"Can we decorate your cast?" she asked Miley, biting her lower lip. "I've been dying to all day! That plain white plaster just doesn't do your sparkly personality justice, Miley."

Kyra, Miley, and JoJo laughed.

"I would love that!" Miley said.

"Great." Grace leapt to her feet in excitement. "Because I bought a set of waterproof paints and a whole bunch of waterproof glitter glue for this very reason. I'll be right back!" Grace ran inside, and the girls sprawled out, gazing up at the sky. It was already getting dark at 8 p.m.; the moon was full, and JoJo could make out a hint of stars.

"I have a fun idea for after cast decorating and movies," JoJo told the others. "What do you think about telling ghost stories later tonight?"

Kyra shivered. "I don't know about that, JoJo! You know how I freak out when I see spiders. Ghosts are like spiders times a thousand."

"Without the creepy legs," added Miley.

"We don't know that!" said Kyra. "Ghosts can look like anything!"

Just at that moment, the girls heard a rustling in the bushes outside the fence surrounding Miley's house.

"What is that?" JoJo reached over and gripped Miley's hand tight, while Kyra hopped into Miley's lounger, shivering hard.

"Probably just a squirrel," Miley said. "They love eating the vine that borders the backyard."

Then there was a loud crash and the sound of the gate's latch popping open—even though JoJo could swear it had been locked. In fact, she remembered Miley's dad double-checking it after he set up the projector! The three friends held their breaths as the gate squealed open slowly . . . then there was the sound of harsh breathing and footsteps coming toward them across the lawn, and then two objects hurled themselves at all three girls just as someone shouted, "Boo!" from the gate's entrance.

Kyra screamed.

Miley screamed.

JoJo screamed.

Then JoJo's face was attacked . . . with kisses! From BowBow!

Kyra leapt out of her chair and flicked on the pool house light. Grace's little brother was standing in front of them, doubled over laughing. Grace was standing behind him toting a big bag and looking sheepish.

"You should have heard yourselves," Grace's brother exclaimed. "You were so freaked out!"

Then Grace's big sister, Megan, stepped in. "Anthony! Get back in the car, you doofus. I'm so sorry," Megan said, turning to the group. "Grace called me and asked me to pick up BowBow and drop her off along with Georgie. Then this little bozo wanted along for the ride, and now I know why!"

JoJo felt her heart slowing to its normal pace.

"It's okay," she told Megan. "I think we'll recover!" She snuggled BowBow closer and turned to Anthony, who was seated cross-legged on the grass with Georgie. "My big brother is the greatest, but I don't have much experience with little brothers!"

"Try little *monsters*," Megan said, laughing. "At least this one. Come on, Anthony— say goodnight to the girls. We've got to head back home."

"I didn't mean to scare you guys," Grace said after they'd left, as she was unpacking her art supplies for Miley's cast. "Megan is so excited about her new driver's license and she loves to take the car out every chance she can get, so I told her it was okay to bring the dogs over. And Anthony is just such a ham. He gets on my nerves." She rolled her eyes.

"He's cute," Miley told her. "I've met Megan, but this was my first exposure to the tiny terror! You're so lucky to have a big family, Grace."

"He would've been cuter if he hadn't nearly made me pee my pants out of fright," Kyra said. "But I sure am glad the dogs are here. Look how cute they're getting along!" Georgie was just a puppy still, and he was wearing the sweetest tie-dyed bandana. "Oh em gee you totally made that, didn't you?" Kyra asked Grace, who nodded proudly.

Even though Georgie was such a tiny pup,

she was still bigger than BowBow, who was full-grown but still only about four pounds! Georgie kept swatting BowBow with her paw, then running in circles around her, then crouching low with her paws on the ground and her rear end in the air.

"Georgie is obsessed," Grace laughed. "She usually isn't so playful with other pups!"

"Well, BowBow is pretty irresistable," JoJo said, smiling at the two dog-friends.

Grace was sitting on the edge of Miley's lounger. "I specifically picked out supplies that wouldn't wear off easily," she told Miley. "I want our messages to you to last the whole six weeks you have that cast."

"Mine's going to be you in a fancy birth-day dress," Kyra exclaimed. "How do you feel about giant tutus?"

"I feel great," said Miley. "Who wouldn't?"

"Well that's good, because I made you one for when you're back up on both your feet," Kyra told her. "But I'm going to draw you in it here, so you have something to look forward to."

"Ohhh, I can't wait to see! The real one *and* the illustration, I mean!"

Kyra got to work while JoJo turned the skating movie on to play in the background. She could totally see why Miley loved the film—the skating was so fun to watch, plus the main character was a strong and sassy athlete who didn't take any of the hockey player's nonsense. When Kyra was finished, JoJo took her place, drawing a giant birthday card on the cast with a special message from her. Then Grace filled in around their drawings with looping flowers and beautiful skates and smiley face emojis and an intricate pattern of layered hearts in all kinds of different colors. When they were done, the cast was a masterpiece.

"I almost never want to take it off," laughed Miley

"*Almost* being the key word," said Grace. "I'm so glad you love it."

"Girls! It's nearly ten," called Miley's mom from inside the house. "Time to wrap it up, or we can put on the movie inside."

"We'll be in soon," Miley told her mom. The movie was just ending anyway. The girls all fake-swooned at the end when—"*finally*," groaned Kyra—the two skaters stopped bickering long enough to admit they were in love and share a kiss.

"Toe pick," JoJo teased Miley as they made their way back inside, the dogs scampering at their heels.

"If only this giant cast were an ice skate," Miley replied.

"But a gorgeous not–ice skate it is!" assured JoJo. "Did you have a nice birthday?"

"The very best, thanks to you," Miley told her quietly. "I really do have the best friends ever. I'm so lucky, JoJo!"

"We all are."

"Girls," Mrs. McKenna broke in, "I set up your sleeping bags in the living room since Miley has trouble getting up and down the stairs. I know it isn't quite as fun as her bedroom—"

"Or as spooky as the basement," contributed Kyra.

"—But it'll be easier for you to get whatever you need from the kitchen." She gave the girls a wink. "I may or may not have put the leftover cake in the bottom shelf of the fridge, just saying."

"What an awesome mom," Grace whispered to JoJo. "More cake? After ten?"

Mrs. McKenna laughed. "On birthdays, anything goes," she told them. Grace blushed—she hadn't realized she'd been speaking loud enough for Miley's mom to hear.

"Whoa!" Miley's dad had popped into the room with an old blanket for BowBow and Georgie to sleep on. "Holy moly," he said. "Now *that* is a work of art!" He knelt down to read the note JoJo had written and admire the illustrations the other girls had drawn. "Almost makes you *want* to break an ankle," he commented. Then he stood, surveying the room. "Girls . . . you do realize you're missing something very important," he said, his tone serious.

"Toothbrushes?" JoJo wanted to know. "Mine's in my bag."

"Uh . . . no," Mr. McKenna said. Then he winked at his wife. "But you should definitely brush your teeth after you're done eating more cake. What I was going to say, though, is that you're missing a blanket fort."

"George." Miley's mom placed a hand on his wrist. "I think we've had enough excitement for the day."

"A blanket fort? What's that?" Grace was squishing up her nose the way she did when she was confused.

"'*What is a blanket fort*'?!?!?!? Slander! Kids these days. Okay, no, this is not acceptable. Now I *have* to build you a blanket fort."

"Agreed," Mrs. McKenna said. "Fine, fine, just make it quick—these girls need their beauty sleep."

Mr. McKenna began ordering them around the room.

"JoJo, grab a chair from the dining table and move it in here. Now stack up some of those big books on the table. And turn over those cushions from the sofa like that, on their side. Good. Hmmm . . . now where should the summit be? Oh! I know, the chandelier . . ."

It went on that way for a while, with the girls—other than Miley—moving pillows around and helping drag old sheets and blankets from the upstairs closet. Finally, it was complete: a giant tent that spanned almost the entire living room! When the girls crawled inside—Miley scooting herself along on her butt—it was like they were in an entirely new world, something totally separate from the rest of Miley's house—their own, private castle. Mr. McKenna had even plugged white lights from the Christmas decorations into a nearby outlet, then had strung them through the entrance to the tent to send a soft glow through its entire interior.

"This is so cool," JoJo said.

"I wish we could stay under here forever," agreed Miley.

They looked over at Grace and Kyra . . . but the two were already sound asleep. Miley and JoJo giggled. "Well, it's getting late," Miley pointed out. "And we've had a long day."

"But we didn't get any extra cake yet!" protested JoJo, trying hard to conceal a giant yawn.

"We can have cake for breakfast," Miley told her. "It's still my birthday weekend!"

"Oh my gosh," JoJo whispered. "Miley, look at that!" She pointed to the far corner of the tent where they'd set up a little nest of blankets for the dogs. BowBow and Georgie were curled up in its center, spooning.

"It's like us—friends for life," Miley said. "Except with more slobber."

"Gross," JoJo told her, just as BowBow yawned, then licked Georgie on the nose. "Okay . . . yeah . . . it's exactly like that."

The girls laughed, then wrapped up in their sleeping bags and began to doze off.

CHAPTER 9

"**G**irls!" JoJo woke up to the sound of Mrs. McKenna's voice and one of BowBow's signature kisses. Despite BowBow's love for Georgie, she'd found her way to JoJo's pillow in the night. "Time to wake up—chocolate chip pancakes with whipped cream and chocolate sauce are coming right up. And there's something special you need to see!" JoJo yawned and stretched. It was so dark under their blanket fort! It felt like the middle of the night.

"What time is it?" Miley asked, from her perch atop a bunch of blankets, her leg raised aloft.

"Ohmygosh, it's 9 a.m.," Kyra informed them. "We slept in!"

"Speak for yourself," JoJo said, rolling back over on her stomach. "Some of us like our beauty sleep." Personally, JoJo liked to sleep in whenever she could.

"Well, I'm going to have pancakes," Grace said, scooping Georgie up and crawling back out of the tent into the living room. JoJo was just dozing off again when Grace popped her head back in.

"You guys," she said excitedly, "Jacob's baking contest is being live-streamed on YouTube!"

"What!" JoJo sat up straight and knocked her head into a blanket, accidentally dislodging it from the cushion that was supporting it and pulling half the fort down over her and BowBow.

"Help!" she shouted. "Man down!" Fortunately, the others had gone to eat pancakes at some point after Grace had, so JoJo was the only one currently lost in a sea of blankets. With Grace's help, she tossed off the giant comforter that threatened to bury her and pulled BowBow from the wreckage.

"That was a close one," she said dramatically to BowBow, who barked her agreement. Then, to Grace, "How did you guys figure out it was being live-streamed?"

"Jacob's mom called Miley's mom," Grace explained, rolling up the cuffs of her oversized, caticorn pajama top. "It's already the final round. Mrs. McKenna didn't want to wake us. But she also said the first three rounds were kinda boring. 'Kids' stuff,' she said."

"Well, we *are* kids," JoJo pointed out. "But I'm glad I got to sleep in, and she's right that Jacob's talent goes way beyond the talent levels of most people our age."

"Less talk, more walk," Grace said, hurrying back toward the kitchen.

"Okay, okay!" JoJo wiped the sleep from her eyes, stretched, then ran after her friend.

When she got to the kitchen, Miley and Kyra were hunched over their plates, shoveling giant forkfuls of chocolate-chip pancake into their mouths, their eyes fixed on the TV mounted directly above the pantry. It was set to YouTube, and there was their friend, creating what looked like . . . a mountain of mush? Still, Jacob moved with a confident ease.

"JoJo, you'll never believe what the final round's challenge is," Miley said, her voice awed.

"What is it?"

"They've been instructed to fix a bunch of smash cakes! You know, smash cakes, like when toddlers smash their first cake? Except in this case the judges did it, and now the contestants have to make an 'after' version that looks almost as good as the 'before.'"

"That's . . . like . . . really hard," Kyra added.

"But," Grace explained, "Jacob already fixed Miley's cake yesterday. Remember how he struggled to make just the right fondant? Now he knows exactly what he's doing."

"I had all of this in mind when I dropped Miley's cake, of course," Mr. McKenna said with a wink.

"This is the best coincidence *ever*," JoJo

exclaimed. "No way the other cakes will look as good as Jacob's."

"He has the hardest one, though," Grace said. "His is the Statue of Liberty!"

"What are the others? Is that a . . . top hat?"

"Yep, with a rabbit coming out. And the other one is a succulent," Miley explained.

"Those all sound tough to me," JoJo told them. "Oh no! Look at those before photos!" Three "before" shots flashed across the screen. In the shots, the cakes were placed on tables next to the contestants: Jacob and another boy and a girl, all about the same age. The tabletops hit below their waists, but the cakes towered over their heads! It looked like an impossible task.

The camera panned over the three contestants. The other boy was bent over his magic hat, his dark brow furrowed in concen-

111

tration. There was an entire rabbit ear missing, and half the cake had crumbled into a landslide. He pulled a tin out of the oven and placed it on a rack to cool, then began mixing powdered sugar with the contents of another bowl—it likely contained water and gelatin and a few other ingredients, JoJo now knew after watching Jacob work his magic the previous day. She guessed he was going to cut a new piece of cake from his tin rather than try to re-shape what had crumbled away, then "stitch" it to the remaining cake with fondant. JoJo couldn't see the girl's face—just the top of her short spiky blond hair as she bent over the frosting she was rolling into long sheets, then slicing and shaping into succulent leaves.

"That's pretty impressive," Miley commented. "Her leaves definitely look as good as the originals."

"Yeah, but Jacob has to make all those folds in Lady Liberty's gown, plus her tiny torch. And I mean, he has to make her look like a person in statue form!" Grace was wringing her hands in panic. "It's not fair! Why did he get the hardest thing?"

"It was a random drawing," Mrs. McKenna explained. "He just had bad luck."

"Okay, but if he nails it, his is going to be incredible," JoJo pointed out. "Since it's the most challenging, it has the ability to win over the judges if he pulls it off."

Miley nodded. "So true."

The girls sipped their orange juice quietly as the final stages of the competition approached.

"Contestants, you have seven minutes," piped a tinny voice through the TV. JoJo was getting nervous. Succulent girl was almost done, and the magic hat was finished except

113

for the embellishments: rabbit ears and a yellow ring lining the edge of the hat. Jacob still had a lot to do. Like, a lot. He was only halfway through molding Lady Liberty, never mind the folds in her gown or the shape of her torch! For now she was mostly a formless blob.

But Jacob worked with the kind of strong, precise focus that meant he was in his zone. And the good news was, the base of the statue was mostly intact—a little bit of shaping detail with a small tool made it look flawless. Jacob just had to add the same level of flawless detail to the statue herself, and that was no easy task with only four minutes left on the clock.

The girls were spellbound. Succulent girl had already placed her succulent cake on the judges' stand. Magic hat guy was just finishing up his hat; but as JoJo looked closely, she could see that his fondant was thin—the

114

yellow ring around the hat was a bit runny, and the rabbit ear was starting to sink in on itself. The boy looked at his cake, shrugged, made some halfhearted efforts at dabbing at it, then brought it over to the judges' stand.

"One minute," one judge called. "And just a reminder that if your cake is not on the judges' stand when the timer rings, you face automatic disqualification." JoJo heard Grace gasp. She grabbed Kyra's hand beside her. Even Mrs. McKenna looked grim.

"Thirty seconds," said the judges. Jacob leaned closer to his statue, curving the flame in her torch just so. Her pronged crown seemed to be holding its shape, thank good-ness. Jacob added one final flourish to the flame, then carried his cake carefully across the floor to the tune of a countdown.

"Ten . . . nine . . . eight . . . ," the audience cheered. Jacob was halfway across the room.

Surely they'd let him participate even if he missed the clock? JoJo wasn't sure.

Jacob placed the cake on the table just as the audience was counting, " . . . three . . . two . . . ONE!"

"You certainly used all of your time," one of the judges said, raising an eyebrow. "Working quickly under pressure is an important quality for a chef to have." JoJo couldn't tell whether that was a compliment or an insult. Had Jacob been working quickly given how hard the task was, or too slowly?

On the screen, the judges began to circle the masterpieces. At Miley's kitchen table, the girls and Miley's parents waited anxiously. Then a tall judge with a long beard stopped smack in front of the magic hat. He leaned over, peering at the yellow frosting that dripped down the side where it was supposed to be ringing the hat. Then, as if it

could no longer take the pressure, one rabbit ear caved in on itself, disappearing inside
the hat!

"Oh no," whispered JoJo. "I want Jacob to
win, but . . . I don't want those other kids to
feel bad!" It was true that the little chef with
the dark hair was upset. A tear was rolling
down his cheek.

"The frosting isn't right," the judge said.
"Let's see how it tastes." He cut into the hat,
taking a big slice for his plate and for the other
judge. JoJo could see that the black frosting of
the hat had seeped into the yellow cake, col-
oring it. That couldn't be good.

The first judge took a big bite.

"Mmm," she said. "Not bad. It looks strange,
but the black-and-yellow cake is better than
the original! It is a bit soft, and the frosting
is running. But it is a very nice cake." The boy
beamed, wiping away his tear.

They moved on to the succulent plant cake.

The bearded judge pulled one of the perfect green sugar leaves right off the cake with his fingers!

"Gross," Miley said, shaking her head.

The judge took a bite and there was a loud *crraaaaack*. Then he put his hand to his mouth. "Ow," he said. "This frosting is too hard to eat. I nearly cracked a tooth!"

Then they moved on to Jacob's cake. Jacob was standing tall, and he was wearing his birthday bomber. But JoJo could tell from the expression on his face that he was nervous!

"The torch is a little off," said the bearded judge. "The whole statue is tilting to the side on its base."

The other judge said, "May I?" When Jacob nodded, she stuck her fork right into Lady Liberty! Then she took a giant bite.

"Oh my," she said, as she chewed. She

handed a fork to the bearded judge. "You must try this." The bearded judged sniffed but took the fork and jammed it into Lady Liberty's dress—the part of the cake Jacob had made from scratch. He chewed and swallowed. His eyes widened.

"This cake," he said, frowning. "It is magnificent!" He threw his arms in the air. "You added raspberry to the center?"

"Yes," explained Jacob. "The cake already had a lemon center, but I didn't have ingredients to re-create that when I was adding to the cake. I thought raspberry would go well with lemon."

"Well, young man," said the man with the beard. "You thought right!"

"And look," said the other judge. "We took two giant bites out of Lady Liberty, and she still stands!" JoJo, Miley, Kyra, and Grace giggled. It was true. Maybe she wasn't perfect, but the statue still stood proudly, even with two giant bites gone! And the bearded man was going back for more!

"I used a framework of long toothpicks to reinforce it," Jacob explained. "I wanted to make sure she wouldn't fall apart."

The judges weren't even listening anymore. They were munching happily on the cake. Finally, one put down his fork.

"We have a winner," he announced, green frosting stuck to his mustache. "Our California Junior Master Pastry Chef is . . . Jacob!" he shouted, squinting at Jacob's name tag.

JoJo and her friends yelled and clapped from where they sat in Miley's kitchen. On TV, Jacob walked over to the other baking contestants and shook their hands, then gave each of them a smile and a hug.

"Jacob is so classy," Grace said.

"Such a Siwanator," JoJo replied. "Even if

he'd lost, I bet you he still would have hugged them and shaken their hands."

"Of course!" Kyra chimed in. "Kindness counts!"

"Someone should tell that to magic hat guy," Miley giggled. The boy was storming off the stage—he even kicked a chair as he went!

"Hmm," said JoJo. "He could use a little Siwanator love. Do you think we should—"

"Noooo," Miley said. "JoJo, you can't teach everyone!"

"Well, Miley," JoJo said, "I hope you had the best birthday ever."

"I did!" Miley said. "But it isn't over yet—where are you going, JoJo? I thought we could go pet Dusty at the stables after breakfast."

JoJo shook her head. "I'm afraid I have work to do," she explained. "After all, we have another party to plan!"

"We do?" Grace looked confused.

"A congratulations party for our Junior Master Pastry Chef!" JoJo exclaimed. "Who's with me?"

"Hear, hear!" shouted her friends.

"After a quick trip to the stables," Miley added, reaching for her crutches.

"Anything you want, birthday girl." JoJo gave her best friend a huge hug. "We'll say hi to Dusty, but then . . . party planning time!"

"Siwanatorz never stop, do they?" asked Mrs. McKenna, her voice tinged with amusement. "Off to the doughnut shop for Doughnut Planning?"

JoJo rubbed her belly and groaned. "Doughnuts might have to wait until Monday," she told Miley's mom. "But planning starts now!"

The other girls burst into laughter. "Let's do it!" Miley said. There was always time to make a friend feel loved.